Wolf H

Arjo's Bike

Roderick Hunt

Illustrated by Alex Brychta

OXFORD
UNIVERSITY PRESS

OXFORD
UNIVERSITY PRESS

Great Clarendon Street, Oxford OX2 6DP

Oxford University Press is a department of the University of Oxford.
It furthers the University's objective of excellence in research, scholarship,
and education by publishing worldwide in

Oxford   New York

Auckland   Cape Town   Dar es Salaam   Hong Kong   Karachi
Kuala Lumpur   Madrid   Melbourne   Mexico City   Nairobi
New Delhi   Shanghai   Taipei   Toronto

With offices in

Argentina   Austria   Brazil   Chile   Czech Republic   France   Greece
Guatemala   Hungary   Italy   Japan   Poland   Portugal   Singapore
South Korea   Switzerland   Thailand   Turkey   Ukraine   Vietnam

Oxford is a registered trade mark of Oxford University Press
in the UK and in certain other countries

British Library Cataloguing in Publication Data

Data available

ISBN-13: 978 0 19 918664 8
ISBN-10: 0-19-918664-2

10

Printed in Hong Kong

Chapter 1

Loz and Gizmo came round to play
with Kat and Arjo. They came on
their bikes. Gizmo's bike was new. He
had it for his birthday.

Gizmo was proud of his new bike.
It was a Tracker. He rode it slowly
round and round. Arjo got on his
little bike and cycled round too.

Arjo's bike was too small for him. It
didn't have gears. It wasn't new when
he first got it.

Gizmo looked at Arjo. 'It's time you had a new bike,' he said.

Arjo grinned. 'I love this old bike,' he said.

Maybe Arjo loved his bike too much.

Chapter 2

Loz and Gizmo wanted to go for a bike ride.

'Do you both want to come?' asked Loz.

Arjo nodded.

'Great!' said Kat.

Mrs Wilson worried about Arjo. She wouldn't let him cycle on the roads on his little bike. 'I don't think it's safe,' she said. 'Besides, he can't hear the traffic.'

Arjo pulled a face. He wanted to go out for a bike ride.

Mrs Wilson had an idea. 'I want to go into town,' she said. 'I'll go on my bike and you can all come with me. We can go along the canal.'

7

The canal went right through the
town. A path went along the bank. It
was safe to cycle on.

Arjo was pleased. He loved riding
his bike.

Chapter 3

There used to be a big factory by the canal. It had been pulled down. There was nothing left, just piles of bricks and bits of wood.

There were some teenagers by the old factory. They had made a ramp out of two big planks and an old oil drum. They were cycling over the ramp.

Mrs Wilson and the children looked
at the ramp. It was blocking the path.
To get past they would have to go
over the grass.

Suddenly, Arjo rode towards the
ramp.

Kat gasped. 'Stop him,' she shouted.

Loz tried to stop him. 'Arjo, come back!' she yelled. They knew Arjo couldn't hear.

Arjo went faster and faster.

'Oh no!' said Mrs Wilson. 'He'll fall in the canal!'

Arjo stood up on his pedals to get more speed. Then his front wheel hit the ramp.

Chapter 4

Arjo went up the ramp like a rocket. He came down the other side. Then he did a skid stop.

He looked back at everyone and grinned.

The teenagers laughed. They clapped and cheered. Kat, Gizmo and Loz cheered too.

Arjo got off his bike. Then he bowed.

Mrs Wilson was angry. She grabbed
Arjo by the arm. She put her face
close to his so he could see her lips.
Then she told him off. Arjo pulled a
face.

Mrs Wilson made him cycle close
to her. 'You see, I'm right not to trust
him,' she said.

'Phew!' said Gizmo. 'I hope I never upset your mum.'

Arjo looked at Kat. 'It was easy,' he said.

'You might have fallen in the canal,' said Kat. She looked at the water. It was the colour of cold coffee. 'You wouldn't want to fall in there,' she said.

Chapter 5

Mrs Wilson had to go to the bank. 'I won't be long,' she said. 'You wait for me here.'

'Can we go back to the ramp and watch?' asked Kat.

'Yes, but no silly tricks,' said Mrs Wilson.

The children went back along the
tow path. The teenagers had tied the
oil drum to a long plank. It was
floating in the middle of the canal.
Another plank went to the other side.
It looked like a narrow bridge.

The children sat and watched. One
of the teenagers walked on to the
planks.

'Come on!' she shouted. 'Who's going to do it?'

The teenagers started cycling over the planks.

'I wouldn't do it,' said Loz. 'It doesn't look safe.'

Chapter 6

Suddenly a boy grabbed Arjo's bike.
He jumped on and rode towards the
canal.

'Stop!' shouted Arjo.

It was too late. The boy rode the
little bike on to the ramp.

'Lift off!' he yelled.

His friends laughed and cheered.

But the rope had come loose. It slipped off the planks. The planks came apart. The oil drum spun like a wheel and shot away.

Arjo's bike and the boy hit the water. There was a shout and a splash.

The boy swam for the bank. Arjo's bike sank like a stone.

Arjo gave a cry. He ran to the edge.
Then he tripped. There was another
splash.

Arjo had fallen in the water.

Chapter 7

Arjo thrashed about in the canal.
One of the teenagers pulled him out.

Arjo stood on the bank. He was
crying.

The teenagers all ran away. They just vanished.

Kat looked at Arjo. 'What's mum going to say?' she said.

Mrs Wilson had plenty to say. She was furious.

'I leave you for five minutes,' she said, 'and this is what happens.'

Mrs Wilson was worried about the dirty water. She took Arjo home and made him have a bath.

Arjo was still upset. His bike was at
the bottom of the canal.

'Can't we get it back?' he said.

'But how?' asked Kat.

Mrs Wilson thought for a bit. Then
she had an idea.

Chapter 8

Mrs Wilson got a long rope. On the end of it was a big hook. 'Where did you get that?' asked Kat.

'From Mr Brown,' said Mrs Wilson. Mr Brown lived next door. He mended cars.

Mrs Wilson took Kat and Arjo back to the canal. Gizmo and Loz went too.

The oil drum was still floating in the water.

'This is the place,' said Gizmo.

Mrs Wilson threw the rope. It sank in the brown water. Everyone pulled. All that came up was some weed.

Mrs Wilson tried again. Everyone pulled. The rope caught something.

'It's coming,' said Gizmo.

Loz peered into the muddy water. 'It's an old pram,' she said.

'This isn't going to be easy,' said Mrs Wilson.

The rope sank again. This time the hook caught on something heavy.

'Pull,' shouted Arjo.

The rope wouldn't move, however hard they pulled.

Chapter 9

Mr Saffrey was out with his dog. He saw Mrs Wilson and the children pulling the rope.

'Can I help?' he asked.

Arjo told him about his bike.

'Oh dear,' said Mr Saffrey. He grabbed the end of the rope and began to pull.

Even when Mr Saffrey pulled too, the rope wouldn't move. 'It's stuck on something heavy,' said Mr Saffrey.

Arjo looked upset. He thought he'd never see his bike again.

'I'll get my car,' said Mr Saffrey. 'I'll back it down here. I can get it quite close. We can tie the rope to my tow bar.'

Arjo grinned. He knew Mr Saffrey would think of something.

Chapter 10

Mr Saffrey had a long rope in his car. He tied the two ropes together. Then he threw the end over the branch of a tree. He tied it to his tow bar.

Mr Saffrey started his car. 'Stand back,' he shouted.

He drove the car forward slowly.
The branch of the tree creaked and
bent.

Then there was a strange noise.
First there was a huge squelch. Then
a whooshing noise. It sounded like
bath water when the plug is pulled
out – only louder.

A huge iron plate rose out of the canal. It was like a giant bath plug. It swung on the end of the rope.

'Stop!' shouted Mrs Wilson.

The whooshing sound grew louder the water began to swirl. It made a whirlpool in the middle of the canal.

Mr Saffrey got out of his car. He looked at the rope. Then he went pale.

'Oh no!' he said. 'We're draining the canal!'

Chapter 11

The water in the canal began to get lower. People stared in surprise.

'Can't we do something?' asked Mrs Wilson.

Mr Saffrey gulped. 'I don't know what we can do,' he said.

Arjo had an idea. He looked at Mr
Saffrey and pointed.

'You could try and put the plug
back,' he said.

'That's a good idea,' said Mr
Saffrey. He got back in his car. Then
he backed it towards the canal.

The giant plug swung on the rope.

Suddenly, the rope snapped. The plug hit the water with a huge splash. Then it sank out of sight.

Everyone looked at the water. The whirlpool was still there.

'It's no good,' said Mr Saffrey. 'I'll have to go and tell someone what's happened.'

Chapter 12

The lock-keeper came and looked at the canal.

'I'm very sorry,' Mr Saffrey said.

'Hmm!' said the lock-keeper.

'Will the whole canal empty out ?' asked Mr Saffrey.

'No,' said the man. 'It's just this bit – about a hundred metres.'

'Oh dear,' said Mr Saffrey. 'I am very sorry.'

'Hmm!' said the man again.

The canal was full of junk. There were trolleys, old bikes, half a car and a wheel barrow. Arjo's bike lay in the mud.

'There's one good thing,' said Gizmo. 'We can get his bike now.'

There was something else in the
canal. It lay in the mud. It was an old
weather vane.

Mr Saffrey was excited. The
children were excited too. They knew
what it was.

'The copper cockerel!' said Mr
Saffrey.

Chapter 13

That's how Wolf Hill School got its weather vane back.

The copper cockerel was on the school roof for years. It went missing in 1980. Thieves climbed on to the roof and stole it. Another cockerel was put up. It wasn't as good as the old one. It was made of iron.

'We'll take the iron one down,' said Mr Saffrey, 'and we'll put the old one back up.'

He had the copper cockerel cleaned and mended.

It was a great day when the copper cockerel was put back. Mr Saffrey held a party in the playground. Parents and pupils who went to the school years ago came.

'Arjo's bike did us a good turn,' said Mr Saffrey.

Chapter 14

Arjo didn't ride his little bike again. His mum and dad bought him a new one for his birthday.

Arjo was excited. His eyes shone. 'Thank you,' he said. 'It's brilliant!'

'Look after it,' said his mum. 'I don't want *this* bike ending up in the canal.'